Rónán and the Mermaid

A Tale of Old Ireland

Rónán and the Mermaid

A TALE OF OLD IRELAND

Marianne McShane

illustrated by Jordi Solano

CANDLEWICK PRESS

ONG AGO IN IRELAND, when fairy folk dwelt in the hills and merfolk swam in the seas, saints and holy men lived in little beehive huts dotted along lonely shores. These huts of wattle and thatch were the first abbeys.

The ancient Abbey of Bangor lay nestled on the edge of the Irish Sea. There the monks worked and prayed, their companions the seagulls flying on the winds and the seals basking on the rocks.

ONE DAY, AFTER A WILD STORM, Brother Declan was searching for driftwood when he came upon a circle of seals keening softly on the sands. In their midst lay a young boy, wisps of seaweed tangled in his hair and his eyes closed tight. He was wrapped in a shawl woven from seagrass, and a silver ring glistened in his outstretched hand.

Declan looked up the beach and down, but there was no one in sight. He gazed over the water and glimpsed a flash of gold that shimmered by the great gray rocks. The old monk rubbed his eyes and looked again but saw only white foam and swirling waves. The lines in his forehead deepened as he remembered the old tales of mermaids and seal people. He gathered the boy in his arms, slipped the ring into the pocket of his cloak, and hurried back to the abbey.

"I found him with the seals," he told the curious monks. And saying no more, he laid the boy on a bed of rushes and tucked the shawl around him.

Brother Finbar kindled the fire till it crackled and sparked, and hung a basin of milk over the flickering flames. Brother Kevin unlaced his pouch of healing herbs and sprinkled a handful onto the frothy white bubbles. The room warmed with the scent of sage and rosemary. Abbot Comgall himself dipped his fingers in a cup of holy water and blessed the child.

Declan blew gently on the milk to cool it and held a spoonful to the boy's lips. With the first sip, the color returned to his cheeks. With the second, he opened his eyes. With the third, he eased himself up. He glanced wildly around and began pulling and tugging at his clothes. Then he sank back on the rushes and sighed in despair.

Declan dug deep into his pocket and held out the ring. The boy's eyes widened. He reached for the ring and clasped it tight. He turned it over in his palm. He wondered at the tiny *L* engraved upon it.

"She gave it to me," he said. "The lady with the golden hair."

And he told them his name was Rónán and that he had been fishing with his father when the storm blew in. They turned back to shore and tried to outrace the wind, but the waves caught them and tossed them out of their boat into the cold, wet darkness.

"My father could hold me no longer. I was swept out of his arms.

"Then the lady came. I thought it was a big fish, but her hair was long and golden, and she sang to me till we reached the shore."

Rónán's eyes closed and his voice grew softer. "She pressed the ring into my hand and told me that one day I would help her."

Brother Finbar and Brother Kevin looked at each other and shook their heads. They thought it was a fever talking. Brother Declan was not so sure. He thought of the sudden flash of gold by the rocks, and he remembered the legend of Líban, the princess turned into a mermaid. But he kept his thoughts to himself.

"Let the boy sleep," he said. "He is feverish and needs rest." Rónán didn't wake till the moon set and the sun rose.

Day by day, the boy's strength returned. Brother Finbar brought him a speckled egg every morning for nourishment. Brother Kevin strewed herbs under his pillow to cure the fever. Brother Declan tied the silver ring on a linen cord and fastened it around Rónán's neck for safekeeping.

In the evenings, Brother Declan would sit by the boy's bed and tell him the old tales while the candle burned low. He told him about selkies, the seal people, who could shed their skins on full-moon nights and take on human shape. He told him about Líban, who was turned into a mermaid when a great lake flooded her home and drowned all who lived there. For three hundred years she had roamed the lonesome seas.

"No one has ever seen her," the old monk said. "But her singing has entered many a dream on quiet moonlit nights."

Rónán's fingers strayed to the silver ring. In his heart he knew it was Líban who had saved him.

As Rónán grew stronger still and his sorrow eased, he began to help with the daily chores. Brother Finbar gave him a basket of willow and showed him where the broody hens hid their eggs under the bushes by the old oak. Rónán set out each morning with his basket swinging on his arm. But when he heard the blackbird singing in the treetops, he would stretch out in the long grass and close his eyes to listen. The brothers ate breakfast late on those days.

Brother Kevin gave him a little clay jar with its very own lid and showed him where the wild herbs grew by the shore. Rónán filled the jar till leaves spilled over the sides. He squeezed the lid on tight and ran down to the water's edge, racing the seagulls and splashing in the waves. But when he heard the seals singing out by the great gray rocks, he would sit down on the wet sand and listen, hoping to hear the mermaid's song.

Brother Declan had seen the boy entranced by the song of the blackbird. He had watched him sit for long hours listening to the seals. And so he gave him the gift of music: a harp he fashioned himself, made from hazel wood and strung with silver. He showed Rónán how to balance it on his knees and cradle it against his shoulder.

Rónán gazed at the harp in wonder, sliding his hand over the polished wood and tracing the flowers and animals carved along the sides. His fingers trembled onto the strings, slipping up and down the length of them. Then he pressed into the silver wires, pulled them toward him, and let go. And when he did, music filled the air, pure and sweet as the peal of crystal bells.

Abbot Comgall himself came to listen.

Rónán kept the harp with him always. His melodies could soothe with the hush of the sleep song, fill the heart with joy, or soften sorrow with the pluck of a single harp string.

When he played under the old oak, the blackbirds sang in the treetops. And when he played by the shore, the seals came up on the sands to listen. But the melody he yearned for was the song of the mermaid.

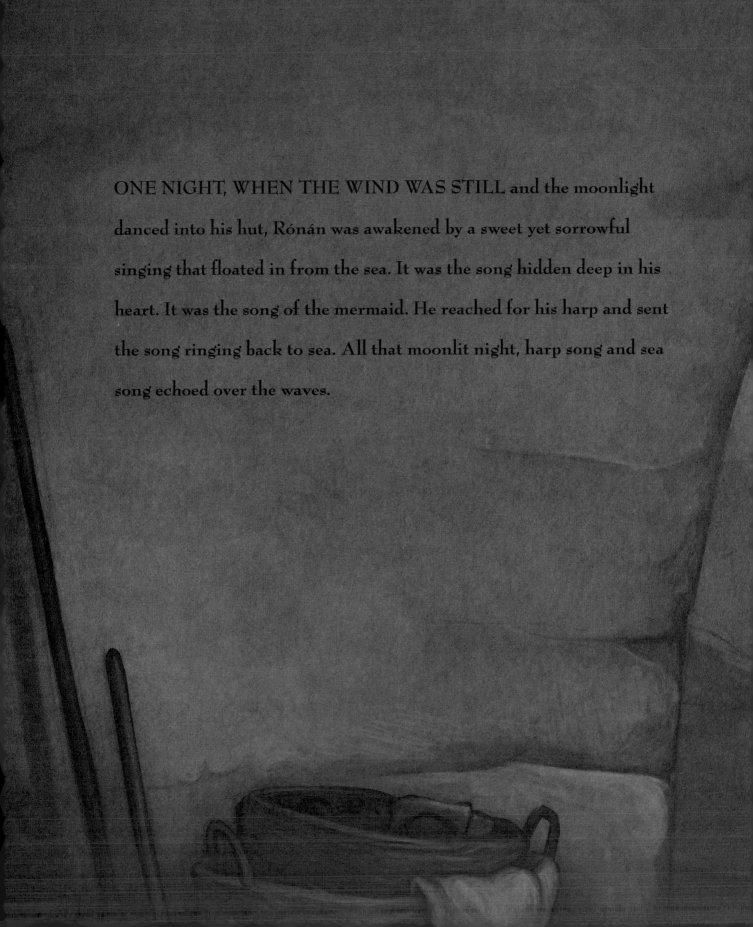

ONE NIGHT, WHEN THE WIND WAS STILL and the moonlight
danced into his hut, Rónán was awakened by a sweet yet sorrowful
singing that floated in from the sea. It was the song hidden deep in his
heart. It was the song of the mermaid. He reached for his harp and sent
the song ringing back to sea. All that moonlit night, harp song and sea
song echoed over the waves.

In the morning, he went to Abbot Comgall.

"Let me row out today and catch fish for our supper."

Comgall understood the longing in the boy's eyes and gave him his blessing.

Rónán tucked the harp into its soft leather bag, stowed it safely in the currach, and rowed out far beyond the great gray rocks, where the seals lay watching. He cast his nets and then began to play his harp. As the notes floated upward, waves rippled to the melody and gulls hovered over the little boat. A lonesome song came in reply, faint at first, then stronger.

With a cry of joy, Rónán let go of his harp and rushed to pull up

his nets. Entangled in the fine mesh was a beautiful girl with long golden

hair and a silvery tail.

"Líban," he murmured.

"Yes," she answered. "Your music has softened my sorrow. Now you

can help me. For three hundred years I have been adrift with no shelter

from the wild seas. Take me to your holy abbot so that I may have his

blessing and find peace."

He leaned over, took a firm grasp, and pulled her into the boat. The little currach pitched from side to side and the harp of hazel wood was flung out onto the water. Rónán watched it sink down to the Land Under Wave and become part of the sea. And though his heart grieved at losing it, there was no sacrifice he would not make to help Líban.

Rónán rowed back as fast as he could, seawater lapping in his boat and Líban floating in it.

Brother Declan and Brother Kevin were waiting on the shore with Abbot Comgall. They too had heard the singing. They watched in wonder as the boy and the mermaid drew closer.

"You are a fisher of souls," Comgall said. And he stepped into the cold waves and blessed Líban. He christened her Muirgen, which means "born of the sea," and in later years she became known as the Mermaid Saint.

RÓNÁN CONTINUED TO FISH EVERY DAY. Líban kept him safe on the sea, and the seals guided him to the best fishing places. He became known as a great fisherman, for his nets were always full and the monks never went hungry.

Brother Declan carved him a new harp in the shape of a mermaid. And Rónán became known as a wondrous harper, for he could soothe with the hush of the sleep song, fill the heart with joy, or soften sorrow with the pluck of a single harp string. But more wonderful still, he could charm the merfolk up from the waves, for when he played his harp on full-moon nights, the selkies danced on the sands and Líban sang her songs of the sea.

Author's Note

Around the year 556, Saint Comgall founded a monastery on the shores of Belfast Lough on the northeastern coast of Ireland. The great Abbey of Bangor, Bangor Mór, soon became known throughout the country for its scholarship and learning, and young men came from every corner of the land to study with the wise abbot.

The *Annals of the Four Masters*, a medieval chronicle of Irish history, tells of a wondrous happening in 558: "In this year was taken the Mermaid, Líban . . . in the net of Beoan, son of Inli, the fisherman of Comhgall of Beannchair." The annals also record that Líban was baptized by Comgall and given the name Muirgen, meaning "born of the sea." This fragment inspired my story of Rónán and the mermaid.

The ancient abbey is long gone, sacked and burned by Viking raiders. But if you go to Bangor today, you will find a new abbey, where wise Comgall is remembered still and Rónán's harp sparkles in a many-colored window. Líban, the Mermaid Saint, floats on a quilt on the transept wall. There she sings forever on the crest of a sea wave.

For my daughter, Catriona, who dances in my
heart like moonlight on sea waves

M. M.

For Ana — for the most wonderful adventure
that's about to begin

J. S.

First edition 2020

Library of Congress Catalog Card Number pending
ISBN 978-1-5362-0022-5

20 21 22 23 24 25 CCP 10 9 8 7 6 5 4 3 2 1

Printed in Shenzhen, Guangdong, China

This book was typeset in Bernhard Modern.
The illustrations were done in pencil, watercolor, and digital media.

Candlewick Press
99 Dover Street
Somerville, Massachusetts 02144

visit us at www.candlewick.com